PAINTING PEPETTE

PEPETTE

JOSETTE

MÈRE AND PÈRE

JULIETTE AND JEANETTE

GRAND-MÈRE AND GRAND-PÈRE

M. DALI

M. PICASSO

M. MATISSE

EIFFEL TOWER

M. CHAGALL

For ma soeur Gail,
whose love of Paris inspired this book
and who continues to inspire me every day.
—LRL

To Joyce and Malcolm Fletcher,
Peter and Alice, with love.
—CF

A TEMPLAR BOOK

First published in the UK in 2016 by Templar Publishing,
part of the Bonnier Publishing Group,
The Plaza, 535 King's Road, London, SW10 0SZ
www.templarco.co.uk
www.bonnierpublishing.com

First published in the U.S. in 2016 by little bee books,
part of the Bonnier Publishing Group

Text copyright © 2016 by Linda Ravin Lodding
Illustrations copyright © 2016 by Bonnier Publishing

1 3 5 7 9 10 8 6 4 2

ISBN 978-1-78370-593-1

Printed in China

PAINTING PEPETTE

written by
LINDA RAVIN LODDING

illustrated by
CLAIRE FLETCHER

ⓣ
templar publishing

Josette Bobette and her rabbit, Pepette,
lived at no.9 Rue Laffette, Paris.

Josette adored Pepette and took her everywhere.

But their favourite thing to do was cuddle on
the window seat in the Bobettes' great room.

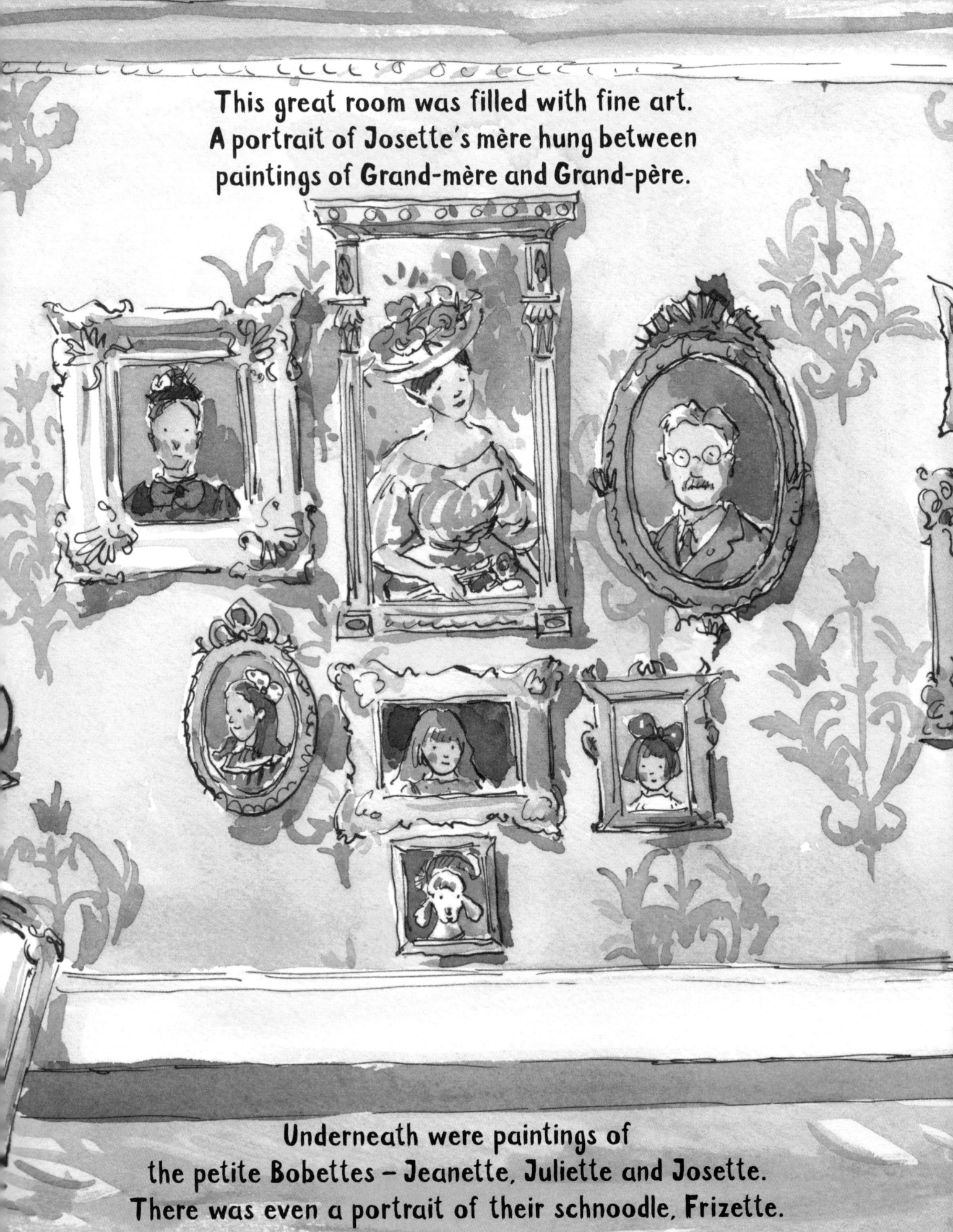

This great room was filled with fine art.
A portrait of Josette's mère hung between
paintings of Grand-mère and Grand-père.

Underneath were paintings of
the petite Bobettes – Jeanette, Juliette and Josette.
There was even a portrait of their schnoodle, Frizette.

One day, Josette noticed something strange.
There was no portrait of **Pepette!**

"We must find an artist to paint
your portrait," said Josette.

"And it has to be
special – just like you!"

So the two friends set off to Montmartre
where the best artists in Paris painted.

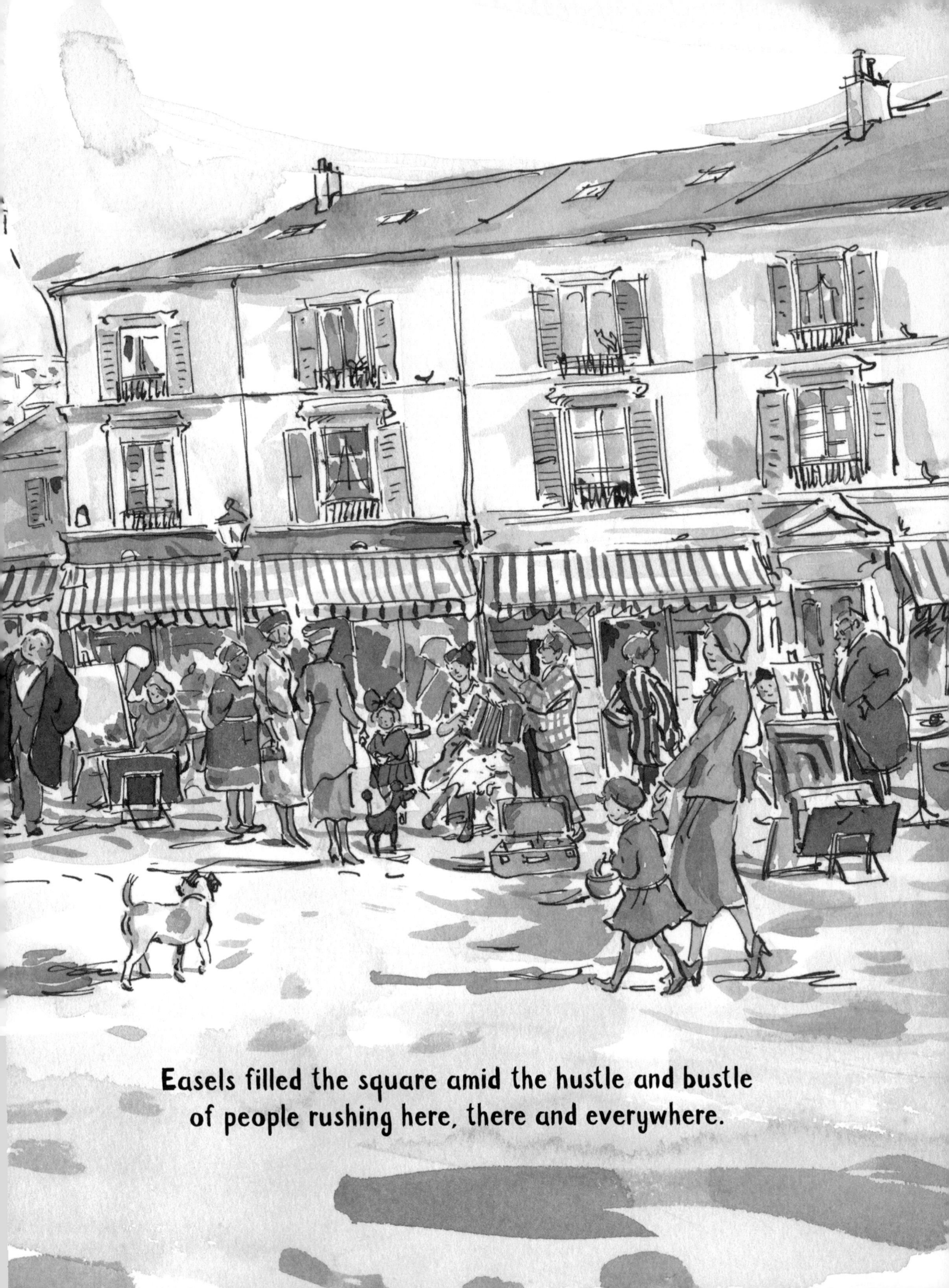

Easels filled the square amid the hustle and bustle
of people rushing here, there and everywhere.

As soon as they turned the corner, a man
in a sailor-striped shirt stopped them.

"THOSE EARS!" he cried.

"Never have I seen such
majestic ears. I *must* paint
this rabbit's portrait!"

Josette noticed Pepette blushing.
Her ears had never been called 'majestic' before.
"Magnifique!" said Josette. "We are looking for an artist."

The painter propped open his easel and filled his canvas with not one, but *two* button noses, and *three* rabbit ears! When he finished, he waved his paintbrush in the air and declared his painting a 'masterpiece'!

"What do you think?" he asked.

"It's nice," said Josette.
"It's just that Pepette has
only one nose and two ears."

And Pepette had to agree.

Just then a man with a moustache as wide as bicycle handlebars strolled by.

"What a divine creature!" he said,
twirling the ends of **Pepette**'s whiskers.

"**Please, I** *must* paint the very
essence of her rabbitness!"

The man painted a most unusual portrait.
"You like?" asked the painter, motioning to his canvas.

Josette stood back.
"It's imaginative," she said,
trying to find just the right words.
"But you painted Pepette quite, well, droopy."

And Pepette had to agree.

Moments later another painter wandered by.
He stopped in his tracks when he spotted Pepette.

"That nose! Like a faint star
twinkling in a misty, velvet night."

As he bowed to Josette, a shock of
black curls flopped over one eye.
"May I paint your friend? My easel is
across the square."

"Pepette would like that!" said Josette.
*Certainly this artist would paint
just the right portrait,* she thought.

Pepette and Josette hopped through the square
until they reached the painter's easel.

More and more people gathered around and looked on as he painted a rabbit... flying through the clouds!

When he had finished, he admired his painting.
"One of my best works!"

"I like the clouds," said Josette. "But Pepette
doesn't like to fly. She's scared of heights."

And Pepette had to agree.

"**THAT RABBIT!**" said another painter.

He peered at Pepette through his round spectacles.
"What a colourful lady – balloon blue,
pansy pink and radish red!"

Was he talking about Pepette?
wondered Josette.

"May I have the honour of showing
the world her colours?"

Josette nodded. She was, after all, quite curious.

When the painter had finished, he wiped his brow
and revealed his work to Josette.

"Ta-da!"

The canvas was filled with splashes,
dashes and dots of bright colour.
Josette considered the painting.
"It's awfully colourful. But Pepette isn't pink."

"Ah, yes," he said.
"But through art we
can see the world
any way we want."

The sun was setting on Paris, and Josette knew it was time to head home.

"Merci," she said to the artists.
"It's been lovely meeting you."

And Pepette had to agree.

That evening, at no. 9 Rue Laffette, Paris,
Josette and Pepette cuddled on the window seat
in the great room.

Josette sighed. She had hoped that Pepette could have
a portrait that showed her wonderfulness – with her
soft grey ears that listened to her when she was sad,
with her heart-shaped nose that twitched when she was
thinking and with her soft arms that held her tight.

She had so wanted Pepette to have the perfect portrait.

Suddenly, Josette realised what she had to do!

She took out her paint and brushes and
painted a picture as special as Pepette.
It was the perfect portrait...

And Pepette had to agree.

Author's note:

*Paris in the 1920s was an exciting and creative city.
Many artists – as well as writers, musicians and fashion
designers – flocked to Paris to work on their craft.
While Josette and Pepette are fictional characters, the artists
Pepette inspires are based on real artists living and working in
Paris at that time: Pablo Picasso, Salvador Dalí,
Marc Chagall and Henri Matisse.*

*Today, Montmartre is still an artsy quarter, but long gone
are the days when this area was home to some of the world's
most renowned artists. Yet, if you use your imagination,
you might still see those artists dart along the cobblestone
streets, pitch their easels to capture the warm Parisian light,
and maybe, just maybe, spot a girl and her beloved rabbit.*

PAINTING
PEPETTE
MUSE OF PARIS